LIVE Borders

3 4144 0102 5886 7

D0247996

MEAN
KITTY

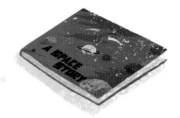

A SPACE
STORY

ROBOT
1080

Clara's Cake

A to
N

POP-UP BOOK of Paris

Paris
POP-
UP

BOOKWORM

Duck

Jungle
Animals

Ben and Benn

The
ELF's
Party

The
Rocket

SHAPES
COLOURS

Hello
Bee!

The First

BOOK OF ART

King

Maths
Puzzles

RUN!

3

FOOD in JAPAN

SNAIL RUSH

The Lemon Story

ROAD TRIP

LONDON

The Sea

ANIMAL STORIES

TRAINS

For my nephew, Bogdan. With love.
I hope you'll grow up to love BOOKS!
C.R.

EGMONT
We bring stories to life

First published in Great Britain 2019 by Egmont UK Limited

The Yellow Building, 1 Nicholas Road, London W11 4AN

www.egmont.co.uk

Copyright © Carolina Rabei 2019

Carolina Rabei has asserted her moral rights.

ISBN 978 1 4052 8848 4

A CIP catalogue record for this title is available from the British Library.

All rights reserved. No part of this publication may be reproduced, stored in a retrieval system, or transmitted,
in any form or by any means, electronic, mechanical, photocopying, recording or otherwise,
without the prior permission of the publisher and copyright owner.

Stay safe online. Any website addresses listed in this book are correct at the time of going to print.
However, Egmont is not responsible for content hosted by third parties.

Egmont takes its responsibility to the planet and its inhabitants very seriously.

We aim to use papers from well-managed forests run by responsible suppliers.

SCOTTISH BORDERS
LIBRARY SERVICES

010258867	
Bertrams	25/01/2019
	£6.99

THE
BOOK
WITHOUT
A STORY

Carolina Rabei

EGMONT

The library is a place that is full of stories.
There are all sorts of stories to read there.

Funny stories,

scary stories, sad stories

and there are also…

... the stories that the books
tell about you!

Oh yes.
When the library closes and the last
librarian has gone home to bed . . .

when there is absolutely
nobody about . . .

all the books come out
and talk to one another.

"My last reader read me on the top of the bus," said Billy the Big Book of Birds.

"My last reader read me at lunch," said Suzy the Space Story. "There are splashes of soup on my pages – yum!"

Sitting way up, on the highest shelf in the library, Dusty sighed sadly. "They put me up here when I arrived so no one has ever read me. I don't even know what kind of book I am."

"There's a girl called Sophie who comes in here all the time – she'd love to read you," said **Marta the Book of Maths Puzzles.**

"But how will she see me if I'm all the way up here?" said Dusty.

"Leave that to me," said Paul the Pop-Up Book of Paris.

The rest of the books made a book ladder so that Paul could climb up to Dusty's shelf.

The next morning, Sophie came into the library with her dad and her little brother Jake.

As she was passing under Dusty's shelf, Paul opened his Eiffel Tower pages and popped Dusty off!

"Good luck!" he said.

Down Dusty **tumbled**, until he landed on the floor – right in front of Sophie.

She picked Dusty up.

And she was **just** about to open him when . . .

she saw her friend Laila.

So instead, Sophie put Dusty on a table and ran over to say hello.

"Bless my bookmarks!" said Billy.

"How can we help him?"

"We can't," said Suzy.

"No one must ever see us move!"

So the other books could only watch
as Sophie's little brother Jake sat down
at the table.

"But Jake's never read **anything!**"
said Marta. "**He just draws!** He won't
even notice poor Dusty is there!"

But then a gust of wind blew in through the open window. Dusty's pages whispered in the breeze, sending out a little cloud of dust.

"Atishoo!" sneezed Jake – and he looked over at Dusty.

And there was a big picture of a dinosaur . . .
just like the one he was drawing!

So Jake pulled Dusty over
and looked at the cover.

Then he turned the page
and saw another dinosaur
picture. And another.

Dusty was full of them!

And next to each picture,
there were words all
about dinosaurs.
His favourite thing in
the whole wide world.

So Jake started to read.

And the more he read, the more the hot, jungly, dinosaur world of **Dusty the Book of Dinosaurs** grew inside his head.

He was still reading when Dad said it was time to leave.

But Jake didn't want to leave, he wanted to keep on reading.

So the librarian explained he could borrow the book
and take it home with him.

Jake read Dusty all the way home
and when he'd finished the book . . .

he started all over again.

And when his friends came round to play, Jake told
them all about the Book of Dinosaurs.

Then he told all of Sophie's friends.
And all his mum and dad's friends too.

When Jake brought Dusty back
to the library the following week, all
the other books wanted to know
about his adventure.

"Did he read you on the top
of the bus?" asked Billy.

"Well, he read me in the car, at the kitchen table, in the bath . . .

and secretly at night," said Dusty.

"Then he shared me with his friends...

it was so much fun!

But I wonder if anyone else will ever want to read me . . ."

"Just look," whispered Marta.
So Dusty did. And he saw…

That everyone did!